D1310605

Flying Feet

James McCann

orca sports

ORCA BOOK PUBLISHERS

Copyright © 2010 James McCann

Library and Archives Canada Cataloguing in Publication

McCann, J. Alfred (James Alfred)
Flying feet / written by James McCann.

(Orca sports)
ISBN 978-1-55469-290-3

I. Title. II. Series: Orca sports

PS8575.C387F59 2010   jC813'.54   C2009-906873-7

First published in the United States, 2010
Library of Congress Control Number: 2009940932

Summary: Jinho wants respect for his skill at tae kwon do, but when he
meets an unscrupulous mixed martial arts trainer, he turns his back on his
sport's code of honor.

Orca Book Publishers gratefully acknowledges the support for its
publishing programs provided by the following agencies: the Government
of Canada through the Canada Book Fund and the Canada Council for the
Arts, and the Province of British Columbia through the BC Arts Council
and the Book Publishing Tax Credit.

Cover design by Teresa Bubela
Cover photography by Getty Images
Author photo by Christina Leist

Orca Book Publishers
PO Box 5626, Stn. B
Victoria, BC Canada
V8R 6S4

Orca Book Publishers
PO Box 468
Custer, WA USA
98240-0468

www.orcabook.com
Printed and bound in Canada.
Printed on 100% PCW recycled paper.

13 12 11 10 • 4 3 2 1

I'd like to dedicate this to my Creative Writing for Children Society classes—both in Vancouver and in Korea. Thanks to you for welcoming me into your culture, and for inspiring me to write a novel that reflects what you taught me.

chapter one

Not a lot of guys enjoy being kicked in the head, but then I'm not like most guys. That feel of a heel smashing my temple, or bent-back toes propelling into my stomach, that's what gets my heart pumping. It's as if my brain is on fire, searching my opponent's body for clues to what he might do next.

I try to remember this as I feel a foot smash into my chest. I fall to the ground and pound the mat with angry fists. I shouldn't be losing, especially not to this guy. He's from the Dragon Dojang and has on a black version of my white uniform. On his back is an embroidered dragon, but no one can see it because we're wearing padding—heavy armor that slows down our movements. We wear it for protection, but as far as I can tell, he's the only one being protected. I can't kick in this stuff.

When he walked into the ring, towering over me, he glanced at me and sneered. I remember this as I get up and bounce on the balls of my feet. My patience is gone, but there's still one more round left. I keep my knees bent and my fists up. I feel his foot swoosh past my ear as I bob left. Dragon has reach, and he's using it to win. I try to move in close. My knee goes up, but the padding slows me down. I snap my leg forward, and he spin-kicks over my foot. All I feel is his heel on my head, and I groan as I fly to the mat. The ref jumps in to give him another point.

I turn away and head to my corner to fix my uniform. What's making this worse is that some guy I've never met is screaming advice at me, while my mom's kind of hiding her eyes. I glance over at her, and she forces a smile. The stranger yells at me to keep my head in the match. He sounds like a crazed hockey parent.

"Mate, this is what you're gonna do," the same guy says as he walks up to me in the ring.

I'm stunned, so I don't say anything. I don't know who this guy is, or what he thinks he's doing, but I listen to him anyway.

"The padding is what's screwing you up. You have hard kicks. If you aim for the gap where the padding is tied, right on the side below the rib cage, you'll have a chance to knock the guy down for good."

"*Chul sa!*" The ref calls me back to the ring. The stranger leaves the ring but keeps his eyes locked on me. I have no time to wonder what that was about, as there's only a few seconds left in the match. The stranger is right. I'm too far behind in points to win. My only hope is to knock the guy out. Little chance of that with all this stupid padding weighing me down.

"*Cha rutt! Kyung yet!*" The ref commands us to bow. I take my eyes off Dragon to show trust. It's a sign of respect before we pummel each other. I see him breathing hard. I am too, but I hide it better. There's no way this guy should be winning.

"*Say jak!*" The ref tells us to begin. I see Dragon's hips twist, and I know he's going for another spin kick. It's the hardest kick we have, and his only chance to win by knockout. I move in fast, taking away the distance he needs for such a move. Punches are worthless in a tournament, but I have such short legs that I can kick this close. I lift one of my knees, but don't kick with that leg. I use it to help me get some height as I jump. With my other leg, I kick out hard, just as he's spinning around. My heel manages to get between his padding, and I feel the flesh just beneath his rib cage. He's caught off guard and knocked to the ground.

"*Go mon!*" the ref yells, and I stop. I walk away as the other guy is checked to make sure he isn't hurt. If he can't stand, I've won by knockdown. The stranger nods and smiles at me. I turn away from the judges and fix my uniform—another show of respect. Dragon staggers up, and the ref calls me back. I know Dragon is struggling, and he's hoping to wait out the few seconds left.

"*Say jak!*" the ref calls, telling us once again to begin. There's only a few seconds left in our bout, but those few seconds can mean win or lose. If Dragon can't stay on his feet, I win. If he manages to ignore the pain, I lose. I try to move in fast, even just one strike, but the judges throw a small sand-filled bag into the ring. The round is over, and I've lost. All because Dragon was able to stay on his feet for a few seconds. If I'd had the chance to kick him, even just once more, he would have gone down. I'm sure of it.

I lower my arms to return to my corner, and Dragon kicks the back of my head.

Maybe he hadn't seen the bag of sand, and he thought the match was still going on. From the corner of my eye, I see the ref rushing to get between us. I only have a few seconds. As my blood boils inside my head, I spin quickly and notice that Dragon's arms are up high. His fingers are open, which is a rookie mistake. I snap my foot, fast this time, and hit his opened hand. He shouts in pain. At least one of his fingers must be broken.

"Disqualified! Illegal move!" the ref yells at me, as he pushes us apart. Dragon is yelling obscenities at me. I'm ready to throw off the padding and give him a real bout. Just then I feel a hand on my back, and I'm yanked to the side.

"Jinho! You will never disgrace my dojang in such a way again!" my master says, bringing the rest of the gymnasium to an abrupt silence. His face is turning beet red, and his grip on me is hard. I yank myself away, throw off the padding and try to remain calm.

"He kicked me after the bag was thrown in!"

"I didn't see the bag!" Dragon yells from behind me.

Now everyone is staring at me, and my mom is nearly in tears from embarrassment. I can't believe that no one is taking my side. There's no way Dragon didn't see the bag. It was a cheap shot, and he knows it! I storm to the change rooms, pushing my way past anyone who dares stand in my way.

chapter two

"Jinho, you let your temper get the better of you. Just apologize. It's part of integrity," Philip says as I get changed after the match.

Philip is a college student who works as Master Jong's lackey, doing chores at the dojang. It bugs me a little when he goes on about the code of tae kwon do. I wonder if he realizes that he isn't Korean. He's wearing a gold medal that he won in the morning's tournament for nineteen- to twenty-two-year-olds.

"There's a pizza party right after the tournament. You're still welcome to come," he says when I don't speak. Right now all I want to do is get dressed and get out of here.

"I'm not a ten-year-old kid who needs a pizza party," I tell him. "I was totally ripped off out there. I could kick that guy's ass—"

He interrupts me by putting his hands on my shoulders. "You broke the rules," he says calmly. His calmness flips my temper into overdrive, and I shrug him off.

"Then the rules suck!" I shout. I want everyone out there to hear me say it too. He has nothing more to say, and I storm out of the building. I'm not even waiting for my mom. What I need is to blow off some steam before I have to go home. If my dad was here, I'm willing to bet he'd have been on my side. He would have patted me on the back and told Master Jong exactly where to go.

I'm walking through downtown Vancouver, heading toward Granville Street. It rained yesterday, so the streets are full of puddles and the air is thick in my lungs. In Korea the cold sky would be sunny, but here gray clouds cover me. It's like this all winter, and I secretly long for hot Korean summer days.

Someone is running up behind me. I figure it must be Kyle, a suck-up from my dojang who does whatever Master Jong asks. When he's behind me, I hear him speak—only it isn't his voice I hear.

"You were ripped off, mate." It's the guy who gave me advice during the match. I look around me for a business to duck into or some sort of crowd to get lost in. I don't know who this guy is, or why he's decided to stalk me. I suddenly realize how alone I am, and how deserted this part of downtown is.

"Thanks," I mutter and keep on walking. I want to quicken my pace, but it makes me feel like a coward.

"It's the padding," he says as he moves in front of me. He's so close that I jerk to a halt and take a step back.

"Okay," I respond, keeping my answers short on purpose. I try and walk around him, but he manages to sidestep and stay in front of me.

"You could have won if you had used your knees." He kicks his knee in the air as if he knows what he's talking about. "Or done a knife strike with your palms."

"You know about tae kwon do?" I ask with a grin on my face. In Korea I started training when I was eight years old. Guys over here train for two years, and they think they're Jackie Chan.

He moves so fast I don't even realize what he's doing. He drops into a walking stance, with both knees bent and feet shoulder-width apart. He steps forward with his far foot and kicks out with his other. In only a few seconds, his heel is gently pressed against my Adam's apple. I'm speechless.

"I know about fighting, and I know about winning," he says, leaving his foot pressed against my throat. "You look like someone who's ready to start winning."

He slowly takes his foot down, and I notice that he keeps his legs ready for another kick. I want to strike back, but the truth is, I'm a little scared of him.

"Why don't you fight back?" he asks, his grin cocky and mocking.

"You're not worth it," I mumble. I try and walk past him. When we're shoulder to shoulder and I'm about to bolt and run, he grabs my arm and holds tight.

"I know I come on a little strong, mate, but that's because I'm passionate about martial arts. I'm offering to help you find that same passion."

As I said before, I'm a little afraid of this guy. He's tough and he shows no fear. He looks at me with complete confidence, and I have little doubt that he could crush me if he wanted to.

"What do you want with me?" I ask.

"To train you," he says, as if he's revealing the cure for cancer. The part of me that's afraid of him wants to say no, but another part of me is curious.

"Yeah, maybe," I mutter as he shoves a business card at me. Before I put it in my pocket, I read the name—Austin. Just Austin. No last name, no address, just a first name, a phone number and an embossed picture of some guy doing a side kick. Kind of shady.

I ignore the warning bells that tell me he can't be trusted. All the things about this guy that scare me are exactly those things that I want to have within myself. Confidence. Indomitable spirit. The very things I've been training for in tae kwon do, but never seem to master. He walks away from me without looking back. I can't help but stare after him and wonder why he picked me.

chapter three

"The problem is, you don't know how to fight bigger guys," Craig tells me during math class the next day at school.

Every time he speaks to me, I remember the first day I came to this school. I hardly spoke any English and was put into a special ESL class. Whenever he saw me, Craig would shout words at me that I didn't understand, and then all his friends would start laughing. This went on until I got angry enough to shove him, and he decked me hard.

The hallway had filled with people coming to watch the fight. People were pointing and laughing at me. I lay on the ground, with Craig standing over me. All his friends were creating a circle around me. I wanted to get up and fight back. I wanted to hit him again. I couldn't. I was too afraid.

Craig still brings out all those emotions in me: fear, rage, shame. I pretend that I'm focusing on my work, but I'm imagining everyone's eyes on me. Whenever I see a note being passed, I can't help but think it's about me. I can't even win a tournament, so how can I win a real fight?

"You gotta stay in close," Craig whispers when Mr. Kelly is writing equations on the whiteboard.

"Seriously, dude?" I growl. "I've been a black belt for longer than you've been in high school."

Craig isn't a small guy, and when he leans in close, he doesn't seem to care if Mr. Kelly is watching. He makes sure to get his face nice and close to mine, and when he speaks, it's slow and deep.

"You want to meet me after school?"

Now I know everyone is watching. The only one not watching is Mr. Kelly, who is probably trying his best to pretend there's nothing going on. Even teachers are afraid of Craig. I curl my hand into a fist, and I imagine striking out at Craig.

"No. Sorry. I didn't mean anything," I say.

"You bet you didn't mean anything," Craig spits out as the bell rings.

Mr. Kelly is going on about homework, but I can hear a tremble in his voice. I can't believe Craig is getting away with this, and I'm too scared to do anything about it. I don't understand why it is that I can't apply what I learn in the dojang to my real life.

"Next time I give you advice," Craig says as he stands up, "you shut up and take it."

I wait until he's left before I start to gather my books.

"If you had met him after school, he wouldn't have been alone," my friend Sara says to me as I stand to leave. She's the only other Korean in my grade, so we tend to hang out a lot.

"Whatever," I say. I don't want to talk about it. For some reason, I start to think about Austin. What would he have done to Craig?

"Are you coming to science class?" Sara asks me. At that moment, I'm more focused on how I lost the tournament and then backed down from Craig—two losses in front of a captive audience.

"First you lose yesterday, and now you chicken out with Craig." Kyle, a guy from my tae kwon do school, has a smirk on his face and a laugh that gives me tiny pin-pricks in my stomach.

"I didn't chicken out. I just don't want to fight him," I reply. "I'm not afraid of him."

"Whatever! We all saw you! You should have seen how white your face went..."

"If I'm such a loser, then why did a martial arts trainer ask me to join his gym?"

"Since when?" asks Jack, another guy I hang out with at school.

"Since yesterday." I reach into my pocket and take out the card as we all start moving toward the science lab. A sense of pride comes over me as I rub my finger over Austin's business card.

"You're making this up," Kyle says, snatching the card from me and showing it to Jack. I can tell by the way Jack is studying the card that he also doesn't believe me.

"Who cares? Can we just get to class?" Sara says.

"Phone him." Kyle's challenge makes my heart start to race. The last thing I want to do is phone this guy. What the hell am I going to say?

I hear the warning bell ring and know that I am going to be late for class.

"You don't get off that easy," Kyle says. "Phone him...or I will." He takes out his cell phone.

I grab the card from his fingers. "No big deal. I'll call him." I take out my cell phone and start dialing.

"Speaker phone," Kyle says, and I hit the speaker button so everyone can hear.

"Hello?" a voice answers.

"Uh, yeah. Is this Austin?" I ask, wishing I sounded as confident as he did. Sara, Kyle and Jack are all staring at me.

"You called my cell phone, so who else would it be? What do you want?"

I consider hanging up right then and there. His voice has an edge to it, and I can almost feel the heel of his foot pressed against my throat. But Kyle is laughing at me and high-fiving Jack as though they've just put one over on me.

"I'm not waiting," Sara says. She joins a group of girls as they pass by us on the way to class.

"Uh, this is Jinho. We met yesterday...," I say, wishing I'd never bragged about this.

"Jinho, mate! Of course! How are you?" As he speaks, his voice changes. He sounds happy to hear from me. A sense of pride swells in me. Kyle shuts up, and Jack's eyes widen.

"Good. Good. Hey, um, that offer for training—how much would it cost me?" I say this for Kyle's and Jack's benefits.

A phone call to ask about price is a legit call, without me having to commit to anything.

Austin laughs. "Cost you? Jingo, we don't make money off our students. Don't worry about the cost. Does that mean we're a go?"

"Yeah, okay," I say. I can't very well say, *Yeah, I was just calling to show off to my friends.*

"Perfect. I have an errand to run in your hood in an hour. You'll be done school, no? Wait for me outside, and I'll swing by and get you."

Austin hangs up fast, almost as if he doesn't want to give me time to change my mind. I close my phone, but instead of feeling good about proving Kyle wrong, I'm wondering what the hell I've gotten myself into.

"How does he know what school you go to?" Jack asks, but I have no answer for him.

chapter four

My mom's friends often call me a Korean parent's dream, since I get straight As and have never skipped a class. Even just skipping on my English tutor makes me feel as though I'm letting my mom down. I have a session right after school, and now I'm wondering what to do. My Canadian friends skip class all the time, and they never think twice about it.

Skipping out on my tutoring session won't be hard, since my mom doesn't speak any English. I'm her translator. If I did get caught, my dad would kill me. Except that he's in Korea, working to support my mom and me in Canada so I can learn English.

The clouds are black in the sky, and the air is heavy with moisture. I try Austin's number, but it goes straight to voice mail. I texted him during science class, but he never responded. I'm waiting for him just outside the school, although I know that I should head home. Kyle and Jack are waiting with me. They still don't fully believe what's happening. Neither do I.

I make sure to breathe—in through the nose and out through the mouth. It's a martial arts technique to calm nerves, and right now I'm so nervous that I keep thinking someone has called my name. I hear the engine before I see the brand-new Camaro pull around the corner. I'm not sure how I know it's Austin, but when the car comes into sight, it just seems like the kind of car he'd drive—loud, powerful, expensive. It pulls up so close that it almost touches me.

"Awesome car!" Kyle says as Austin rolls down the passenger-side window.

"Come on. I don't have much time." He motions for me to get into the car.

I climb in, after pushing Kyle out of the way. I'm being all casual about it, as if this is no big deal. I try to say hi, but I'm so worried that I'll sound like a geek that I stay silent. Austin doesn't face me. He's wearing dark sunglasses, so I can't see his eyes. It's a bit weird, considering there's no sun.

We speed off down the street. I'm not sure where we are going, and I know that I'm breaking some very basic laws of life. Skipping a tutoring session to go off with a stranger, without letting a single person know where I am. I have my cell phone, but will I really be able to call anyone if I need to? I consider texting Sara, but she'd go straight to a teacher.

"You did the right thing," Austin says to me, finally breaking the silence and slowing down as he pulls south onto Oak Street.

"Okay," I say, wishing I could sound as if this was no big deal.

"Before I take you to the dojang, we have to make a stop."

I nod, remembering that he had an errand. I wonder what it might be. We drive down Oak until we hit Marine, where Austin takes a left. Neither of us is speaking, and I'm starting to get nervous. It isn't until we stop in what looks like an industrial district that I realize things could get ugly.

There's a guy standing on the street, wearing a black biker jacket and a red bandanna. He's scruffy, and his hair and beard are wild. Even from where I am, I can see that his knuckles are scarred. He nods at Austin as if they know each other.

"You coming?" Austin asks. There's an edge to his voice.

I don't say anything. I want to say no, and I'm wishing that I had gone to tutoring. Before I can respond, Austin asks, "You're not chicken, are you?"

I suddenly feel the same way I did when Craig was in my face. Part of me wants to get out of the car and be the tough guy, but an even bigger part of me is terrified. Austin opens the car door and steps out. He moves with a confident swagger, with his chest out and shoulders back. He's the same height as the biker, but half his bulk.

"Got the cash?" Austin asks. It doesn't sound like a question.

"You'll get the cash when I want to give you the cash," the biker tells him calmly.

I want to run. Craig is scary, but this guy is dangerous. I can feel my legs start to shake, even though I'm a good distance away and still inside the car. I want to lock the doors, but I wonder if we need to be ready for a quick getaway.

"You were man enough to make the bet, you should be man enough to pay the debt," Austin finally says.

The biker's eyes grow wide, and he steps forward. I start to edge over to the driver's seat, so I can be ready to start the car and drive off. Austin doesn't move. He doesn't smile, nor does he break eye contact with the biker.

"You may wanna get in your toy car and get outta my face." The biker speaks each word through gritted teeth.

Austin throws a punch, but the biker easily ducks underneath. As he does, he brings his knuckles into Austin's stomach, and I hear a grunt as Austin drops to the ground.

"Jingo!" Austin yells. The biker grabs him by his hair and hauls off to strike again. I'm frozen as I watch Austin get hit in the face. I slide over to the driver's seat and put my hand on the keys. Maybe I should drive off and get help, but my muscles freeze, and I can't seem to move. My cell phone is in my pocket, but if I call 9-1-1, I'll get in trouble too.

That's when I realize just how abandoned this neighborhood is. The buildings around us have boarded-up windows and were probably closed down long ago. Where there were once lawns, there are now long yellow weeds. Even if someone did happen by, they would probably avoid the fight. Once this biker is done with Austin, will he start on me?

I open up the car door and try to calm my breathing. In through the nose, out through the mouth. You're a black belt... you don't have to be afraid, I tell myself as I focus on my training. The biker is really laying into Austin, who seemed so tough moments earlier. I put one foot on the ground and then the other. I step out of the car and close the door. I mean to slam it to get the biker's attention, so that I'll appear unafraid, but I wind up closing it so silently that it is almost like an apology.

Austin is on the ground, huddled with his hands over his head and his stomach pressed against the ground. The biker is kicking him hard, and Austin manages to turn his face to me. Instead of the plea for help I'm expecting, he winks and smiles.

Austin kicks out while still on the ground and catches the biker directly between the legs. As the biker falls to the cement,

Austin does a backward handspring to his feet. Grabbing the biker's head, he smashes it against his knee and stands victorious over his opponent.

"I was starting to doubt you," Austin says to me, and I wonder if this was all just a test.

"I was, uh, just coming to help," I stammer, hoping my voice doesn't sound as cowardly as I feel.

Austin reaches into the biker's jacket and finds a wallet. He opens it and removes the cash, quickly counting a few bills in his hands. The biker groans.

"I'm coming back tomorrow, and, one way or another, you're paying the rest," he says to the biker after giving him a swift kick in his side. Then to me he barks, "Get back in the car."

I do as he says, once again feeling admiration. Austin drives away, not even looking in the mirror to see how badly his face is cut and bruised.

chapter five

"You've never been in a fight." Austin is telling me what he knows, not asking a question.

I correct him, thinking of all the tournaments and the sparring I've done in class. "I've been in lots of fights."

"No." Austin laughs. "You have not. Fighting with rules and padding is fun. It's like a game of tag. Children play tag. A real fight is scary, because it will either make you a man or completely break you."

I can feel my cheeks burning a little from embarrassment. He's right. I have never been in a real fight. Master Jong taught us not to use our skills outside the dojang, and I have always walked away from confrontations. How can I be proud of this, when I know that I walked not because I was honoring my training, but because I was afraid?

"Get over it," Austin says as if he knows what I'm thinking. How does he do that?

"What?" I ask.

"Yourself, for one thing. So what if the guy hits you? Maybe he breaks your nose, or maybe he chips a tooth? You heal. Walk away from a fight, and that kind of shame lives with you the rest of your life."

As we drive back toward Oak, I think about Craig and how he had challenged me. What's the worst thing he could have done? I vow never to let anyone intimidate me again.

"We have to make another stop," Austin says.

A voice inside my head asks why. I want to know where we are and what is going to happen, but nothing comes out of my mouth. We've driven only a short distance and are now in a neighborhood of pruned trees and freshly mowed lawns. We park in front of a house with whitewashed walls and stone trim. It takes up three lots. Surrounding it is a tall iron fence with barbed wire at the top.

Austin gets out of the car and motions me to follow him to the gate, where he pushes a buzzer.

"What?" The voice sounds angry. I immediately regret not going home.

"It's Austin." I notice that he doesn't sound as confident. There may even be a touch of fear in his voice. He has the same look in his eyes that I must have had when I backed down from Craig.

There's a loud buzz and the gate slowly starts moving. It makes me think of those old prison movies, where the new inmate is being let into the compound. All we're missing are the shackles and the jeers from other inmates. I follow Austin, who is now walking with a slightly bent posture, his hands tucked into his pockets. I can't help but wonder why he's acting so submissive.

I try to stay close to Austin, though I don't feel as safe with him as I had moments earlier. We walk a winding path until we come to a large wooden door that's been left ajar. As we approach the house, I can hear heavy guitar and drums, like the old-school heavy metal from my dad's generation. I can almost hear my dad's disapproving voice.

"Don't speak unless I tell you to," Austin says as we walk into the house.

There's very little furniture, and the walls are white and bare. No pictures, no rugs. Nothing to suggest that someone lives here. A marble staircase leads from the entrance to the upstairs.

"Do you understand respect?" Austin asks me.

"Yeah." I nod, trying to think about what my master had taught me. Respect is in how you treat someone. Kind acts show you are thinking of the other person first.

"Fear," Austin tells me, "is another name for respect. If someone fears you, they respect you. No matter what happens, that's the lesson you are here to learn."

We walk down a long hallway and through patio doors that lead to an out-door pool. Five guys wearing sweatpants are standing around, bare-chested. A cool breeze ripples the pool, and clouds still cover the sky, yet all these guys are sweating. As we get closer, I notice that Austin's shoulders slump even more and he's staring at the ground. He's acting like a beaten dog.

"Did you get my cash?" one of the men asks. He's easily six feet tall, with broad shoulders. His head is shaved, and there is a scar that runs from the top of his head to his right eye. I can't help but stare at it.

"You looking at me?" the man asks me gruffly, as Austin throws the biker's wad of cash on the table.

"No," I start to say, but I'm cut off by a sharp look from Austin. The man smiles and walks up to me. That's when I realize my lesson is about to begin.

chapter six

"Respect through fear," Austin whispers in my ear as he walks back into the house.

I start to panic as the men surround me. I look for a way to get out, but I'm now in the center of a circle. I tell myself that nothing is going to happen. I'm just a kid. They must know they'll go to jail if they beat me up.

"Do you know who I am?" the scarred man asks me.

"No, sir." I bow. That's how I would address Master Jong, with complete respect.

"Sir." He spits as he laughs in my face. "What style are you?"

"Tae kwon do." For some reason, I'm embarrassed as I say it.

"Are you any good?"

"I guess" is all I can muster. I even shrug my shoulders as I say it. I look for Austin, but can't see him. This is the first time I'm not wishing I could be just like him. I can't believe he walked away like a coward.

"What belt are you?"

"First dan black," I tell him in almost a whisper. I remember that I have a cell phone in my pocket, and I realize how useless it is in an emergency such as this.

The scarred man grabs the back of my jacket, the same way someone might grab a mongrel by its scruff.

"Either you go to a joke school that gives away black belts for free, or you're lying to me."

The scarred man steps back into line to complete the circle. I know this test from martial arts class, where each man throws a punch or a kick and the one in the center has to defend himself. I'm very good at it.

I feel a kick to my lower spine, and my knees collapse under me. As I go down, there's a knee in my chest and a hard punch just under my rib cage. They're coming from all over and all at once. My instinct is to curl up into a ball and protect myself. I know for certain that this is not the same exercise as in class.

As soon as I pull my arms over my head, one of the men leaps on me. He grabs me from underneath and flips me onto my back. I hit my head on the cement deck, and I'm lifted back to my feet. There's a punch to my gut, and I know now that this isn't going to end well. I struggle a bit, but that just seems to make the guy hold me tighter. I feel a burning in the pit of my stomach as I get angry. First at myself, then at Austin, then at these guys.

There's a blood rush in my head that makes me react.

I bring my knee up into the gut of the guy who's holding me by the chest. He loses some air, and I feel his grip weaken. I step back and kick out with my heel, sending him to the ground. I know there's a guy behind me, so I kick back, kind of the way a donkey kicks, and slightly turn my head to see where the kick is going. I manage to get a guy in the face. The scarred man suddenly tackles me and pins me to the ground. He's so strong that I can't toss him off of me. He's got his legs wrapped around my waist and an arm pressed against my windpipe.

"As far as you are concerned, I don't exist. All that matters is that you show me respect," he says.

He gets off me, and I hear him call Austin. The others all walk away, and pain floods my entire body. I let out a few choking coughs.

"He'll do," the scarred man says to Austin, who grabs my arms and hoists me up. I don't dare look back as we head for the door.

"Everyone has someone they respect," Austin tells me as we walk away. "Even him. Even me. And now, so do you."

chapter seven

The drive home is quiet and very uncomfortable. There's an SUV behind us, and its headlights are almost blinding, it's so close. That's what I try to focus on. I'm willing to try anything to take me out of the moment. I squeeze my arms together tightly over my chest and press myself into the car door. One of my legs is shaking. I wish there was someone I could talk to about what has just happened. There isn't.

I know that if I tell my mom, she'll get scared and probably send me back to Korea to be with my dad. He'll be disappointed, and I'll wind up in a private school, working twice as hard as I do now. If I tell anyone else, they'll just tell my mom. Nope. This one I have to figure out on my own.

We turn another corner as we near my house. The SUV turns with us, and it's still tailgating us. It doesn't occur to me yet that I haven't given Austin directions, nor have I ever told him where I live. He just seems to know. I'm not sure how much of a coincidence it was that we met the way we did.

"I'm sorry, mate. I should have warned you that might happen."

I want to say *Screw you*, but I'm too scared. "No worries," I mumble instead. After tonight, I'm losing his number and never calling again.

"I went through the same thing," he says with a bit of pride in his voice, "but I never had the guts to fight back. You have spirit. I'm impressed."

For a moment, I feel a tingle of satisfaction at his praise. I have to remind myself that he almost got me killed.

"The boss is impressed too," Austin continues. "With a club like ours, we have to make sure you can handle it."

My leg stops shaking, and I'm calming down a little. My grip loosens around my chest as I try to sit up straight. There's a sharp pain in my ribs that reminds me to be careful.

"That was a pretty harsh test," I say, forcing the words out. My throat feels dry, like I have the flu.

Austin laughs. Not a sorrowful chuckle, or a sarcastic snicker, but a full-out hoot as though he's watching some comedy show.

"Mate, I love your spirit! Before I came to this club, I was kind of like you. I mumbled when I spoke. I didn't look people in the eyes, and I did everything that my parents asked of me. Everyone loved me"—Austin turns to face me—"except for me."

His eyes stay locked on me for a moment and then return to watching the road.

We pull over about a block from my house, with the SUV's headlights still filling the Camaro's cab.

"Perseverance, indomitable spirit, courage, courtesy and self-control. I know the code of tae kwon do, because I follow it. The trouble with your school isn't the teaching, it's the interpretation."

I'm caught off guard by how much he knows about martial arts. He shuts off the car and pulls the key from the ignition.

"Look, mate, I'm not going to say I'm sorry about what happened tonight. What I did will make you stronger, and that's a good thing."

Austin throws the keys into my lap and then pops his door open.

"In my world, we're rewarded when we do well. Take the car tonight, drive it to school, feel what it means to be a winner. I'll meet you after school and take you to the gym."

As he's getting out of the car, I tell myself to throw the keys back to him. The car ties me to him. It means I have to see him again. This is a guy I should be walking away from, but for some reason I can't. I watch in the rearview mirror as Austin gets into the waiting SUV. I sit in the car for a while, my aching body pressed against the leather seat, my hands clutching the keys.

chapter eight

I leave the car parked where it is and walk home. I don't want my mom seeing it and asking a lot of questions. It's now past eleven o'clock on a school night, but I'm not worried about getting in trouble. This is when I'd normally be finished with my English tutoring.

I go inside quietly and hear my mom call hello in Korean, *"Anyong haseo!"*

"Haseo!" I call back as I kick off my shoes. We always speak Korean at home—

my mom's English is pretty bad. I can barely stand as I limp toward the kitchen, but I know she'll just think I'm acting like a lazy teenager who doesn't stand up straight. I add a shuffle to my feet and stare at the floor, nodding my head only slightly as a bow.

She tells me there's a message for me on the machine, and that it sounds like my tutor. I pick up the phone and dial for the messages. A computerized voice tells me the call came ten minutes after my lesson should have started. He and I usually meet at the library near school, so that he can meet with another student right after.

"He was late. Called to say he's sorry," I tell my mom. I think this may be the first time I have ever lied to her. I'm worried she's going to know I'm not being honest.

"Master Jong called also," she says. Now I know I'm busted. When my mom gets really angry, she doesn't even ask questions. She just makes statements. She knows that I understand what she wants to know. In this case, she wants to know why I missed tae kwon do.

I should tell her what happened. I made a mistake and screwed up. I never should have gone off with Austin, and I never should have believed him that he was some "special" trainer. But I know I'll be in big trouble, and she isn't going to understand. Besides, if I'm never going back, then why should I say anything now?

"I wasn't feeling well, so I stayed at the library to study," I tell her. It helps that I'm a straight-A student and that I study a lot. If there's one thing that makes a Korean mom proud, it's a son who wants to excel.

A wave of relief washes over me as she nods and places two bowls on the table, one of kimchi and the other of rice. I can smell the bulgogi cooking as I erase the tutor's message. He said he waited for me and will be charging me for canceling without notice. I figure I can come up with the cash and pay him at tomorrow's lesson.

After dinner I rush upstairs to my room, where I fall onto my bed and finally let myself experience the pain. I'm thankful that at least they left my face alone, so my mother won't ask what happened. I want to phone the police. After all, how hard can Austin be to track down? I have his car.

My computer makes a beeping noise. I still have three hours of homework to do before I can go to bed. I get up and sit at my computer. Tapping the space bar on my MacBook, the screen wakes up and I see a message from Kyle.

How was training?

I absently rub my hands over my chest and cringe at the pain. It even hurts when my shirt rubs against the bruises. Sooner or later, I'll have to admit that I don't really have some special trainer and suffer the embarrassment of being called a liar. I wonder if I should tell Kyle now.

It was hardcore, I type into the message box.

chapter nine

There's the problem of the car. It will take me sixty minutes to get to school by bus, but instead of hustling, I'm standing on the street staring at the Camaro. It rained last night, and there are perfect beads of water scattered on the red paint. I suddenly realize that I'm standing in a puddle as the water soaks into my runners.

I get into the car and decide that it's better to get Austin to meet me at school, where there are lots of people, than for me to either take the car back to him or have him show up at my house. I remind myself that he knows where I live.

I put the car into Drive and press the gas. It lurches forward, and I hit the brake. I'm inches from the car in front of me. The Camaro is definitely not like my mom's Escort. Gently, I back up a little and then put the car back into Drive. It wouldn't be that big a deal if I drove it a few extra blocks, just to get a feel for it. After all, when will I ever get to drive a car like this again?

The roads are slippery, and sometimes the Camaro skids when I press the gas pedal too hard. Overall, it's an easy car to drive, and I start to feel pretty cool. I press the button that rolls the window down and rest my elbow on the door.

"Cool car!" I hear a girl yell next to me.

I turn and see a car full of girls. I recognize the driver from school. The passenger is a cute blond who's resting her head on her arms in the open window. She's smiling at me.

"Thanks," I say.

"You go to King George, right? I think I've seen you around."

"Uh, yeah." I wish I could think of something else to say. Girls never go out of their way to talk to me.

"Want to drive me to school?" she asks as we pull up to a red light. I realize that I have to think fast. If I say no, she'll never talk to me again. Does it matter that this isn't actually my car?

"Okay," I say to her. Unbelievable. It seems unreal when I watch her hop out of her car and run around to my passenger door. Her friends are all laughing at her.

The light turns green as she's doing up her seatbelt. I start to drive and catch her looking around the interior with wide eyes.

"Is this your dad's car?" she asks.

"No. It's...a friend's."

"Can we go for a ride before we go to school?" she asks me as we pull up to another red light. I'm about to turn left onto Denman from Georgia Street.

"We could do the Stanley Park loop if you want," I suggest. Can't hurt to do one loop, I figure.

"How fast can this thing go?" She flashes me a big smile. The light turns green, and I gun it. Truth is, I wasn't really sure how fast it might go. There's a loud squeal, and we jet off. I feel my body compress against the seat, and the girl screams in delight. I immediately take my foot off the gas and slow down, checking my mirrors for cops without being too obvious.

I enter the park, and she starts fiddling with the radio. She finds some station that's playing dance mixes...not really my style. I realize that I don't even know her name, and she hasn't asked for mine. I'm circling through an area where you can see the mountains and the water, wondering if I should say anything.

After a quick drive around the park, I still haven't asked her name. We head to school, and I notice that I've got only ten minutes before classes start. There's no way I'm parking in the school lot, where everyone will see me with this car. I'm in too deep, and I need to get out.

There's one spot by a meter a few blocks from school, and I start to parallel park. It will mean rushing out to plug the meter every two hours, but I gotta do it.

"We're, like, three blocks from school," the girl says coldly.

"There may be no spaces in the student lot, and this one is open," I say, as though that might be true. The lot is small, but not very many students have cars of their own. There's always a spot available.

"I did not get in your car to walk three blocks to school. Drive me to the door at least."

I wish that I hadn't been so eager to show off. I could just say no, but as she stares at me, I find myself pulling out and heading to the school. She's silent now, and I'm guessing I've erased my chances of finding out her name and her number. We're so close to the first buzzer that there aren't very many students outside. It's easy to find parking in the student lot, though I still pull into the spot that's farthest from the doors. The girl sighs and shakes her head, jumping from the car before I say anything.

"See you," she calls back to me as she rushes to get inside. I see her friends waiting for her on the steps, and I can tell by the tone of her voice that we won't be hanging out anytime soon.

I step out of the Camaro and jog for the door. I can hear the first buzzer now but stop in my tracks when I see Craig and his buddies standing outside the doors. They're finishing a smoke and eyeing my car.

"Nice ride," Craig says. Now I know that I have to get rid of this car sooner rather than later.

chapter ten

We're playing basketball in gym class. Shirts against skins. I stand in line, waiting while everyone gets picked for a team. I'm hoping for shirts, so I won't have to explain the bruises.

"Jinho!" Carl points at me. Crap. I'm skins.

Normally, I have no problem taking off my shirt. Even though I'm skinnier than most guys my age, thanks to tae kwon do

I am quite muscular. I start to lift my shirt but stop and casually say, "Hey, Nigel, want to switch sides with me?"

"No way," Nigel answers, his face scrunching with embarrassment. I can tell none of the other guys want to either. Bunch of skinny TV addicts whose only exercise is this class. Guess they figure if they keep their shirts on, no one will figure out they have no muscle. They all avoid eye contact, so I start to lift my shirt again. Craig puts his hand on my arm, and I stop.

"I'll switch with you," he tells me.

"Really?" I'm surprised.

"Do you want me to change my mind?" He doesn't wait for an answer. He just pulls up his shirt and walks over to Carl, who glares at me for giving him Craig. I walk over to my team and wonder what's going on. It's almost as if he knows about the fight, but how could he?

I take my position as shooting guard, with Carl covering me. I see Craig walk to Carl, pat his back and tell him to switch positions. Carl doesn't argue, but again gives me a glare. I'm not sure what's up Craig's ass, but I decide that I'm not going to let him push me around. I concentrate on watching Jack and Carl go for the jump as Coach Harvey throws the ball. Jack gets the tip, and he's fast getting near the key. I'm trying to get clear, but I've got Craig covering me. He's aggressive, always pushing into my space. A few times he steps on my toes, and I want to call a foul on him. I don't, only because it would guarantee me a meeting after school with him.

"Who punished you?" Craig asks as the ball is taken from my team and dribbled toward my basket.

"What?" I ask as I try to move around him. He's using his bulk to really block me. I wish the teacher would pay attention and call the foul.

"The bruises. I noticed them as you were taking off your shirt. None on your face, all on your chest and back. Someone wanted you to be able to hide them."

Jack gets the ball and throws it to Tommy, who's just behind me. Tommy dribbles a few feet, passes to me, and I dance around Craig. I manage to make it and take a shot. As I jump up, Craig moves in with an elbow to my gut. He hits one of my sore spots and I go down.

"Foul!" Coach Harvey yells. Finally.

"It was an accident," Craig says in a way that tells me I'd better agree that it wasn't done on purpose.

I stand and think about the men who beat me up last night. I remember feeling helpless, and then angry. I'm not feeling any fear now, just that same kind of anger. I walk up to Craig and put my face in his. He doesn't know where I got the bruises, but he knows enough to understand that they mean bad news. That I mean bad news.

"I'll take the foul," I say.

I walk to the top of the key and bounce the ball a few times. I look at the hoop and ignore the pain I feel in my gut. I close my eyes for a second, breathe steadily and imagine the ball swooshing through the net. As I open my eyes I take the shot, watching the ball fly through the air.

When it hits the basket, there's a clanging noise as it bounces off one side of the rim, then the other, rests for a split second and then falls to the floor without going in.

"Tough break," Jack says as we all reposition to continue the game. "Next time just ignore Craig. Who cares, man."

I'm back in position with Craig covering me. Carl gets the tip, and I'm on defense. This time I don't even try to get the ball, or care who has it. I'm concentrating only on Craig, so he can't get the ball.

"Saw you park that Camaro in the lot," he tells me. "You're into something over your head."

"I have a new tutor," I say, hoping he doesn't press for an explanation.

"And he gave you a car? And those bruises?"

I don't say anything. Even I know it sounds crazy. Why would my tutor give me his car? Coach Harvey whistles as a basket is scored on my team. I hear Jack yell at me to stay in the game, but Craig and I are locked in a stare-down.

"Careful," Craig tells me. "No one is that generous without good reason."

As we all start walking back to our positions, I realize that I have to agree with Craig. Austin has been bad news from the start, and I'm already in deeper than I should be.

"Coach, I'm not feeling well," I say as I walk off the court.

"Okay, Jinho. Go to the nurse's office," he says.

I go to the change rooms and get back into my street clothes. I skip the shower and head for the school exit. I take out my cell phone and punch in Austin's number. I practice in my head what I'm going to say.

"Jingo! Glad you called. I need to pick up the car ASAP to check out a potential fighter for our club. Where are you?"

I can't believe how direct he is. I stumble for words.

"I'm at school...," I start to say. I want to add, *You can pick up your car and go screw yourself*, but all I manage is, "Can you get your car?"

"On my way," Austin says. He clicks off as the rain starts to fall.

chapter eleven

I'm so nervous that I start tapping my foot
without even realizing that I'm doing it.
I lean against the school wall, staring at
the Camaro parked in the lot not ten feet
from me. Everyone who walks by stares at
it, and then they glance at me. Girls smile
and linger a little. Guys nod and say things
like "Nice ride."

A black Mustang pulls in behind the
Camaro. The driver is one of the guys who
fought me yesterday. I feel all my muscles

go taut as a knot forms in my stomach. Austin is in the passenger seat, and he gets out to greet me.

"Jingo! Why are you out in the rain? Let's get inside the Camaro and talk."

He holds out his hand, and I toss him the keys. I should tell him *no way* and go back into the school, but he's already sitting in the driver's seat. Without a word, I open the door and get into the passenger seat. The Mustang squeals away.

"You took good care of her," Austin says.

"Yeah, I made sure no one touched her." I don't know what else to say. I wonder if I'll ever have the confidence to say what's on my mind like he does. *I never should have called you, and I shouldn't be here*, is what I should be saying.

"And?" Austin asks. I wonder again if he can read my thoughts.

I shrug.

"C'mon, mate! You're a seventeen-year-old guy, and you show up to school in this car? What did people say?"

"Some girl asked for a ride to school,"

I blurt out. I don't look at him, but I know he's smiling at me. The car is moving, and now I know I'm stuck again.

"Jingo, that's what I want to hear!"

I don't say anything. The fact that he knows so much about me is starting to creep me out a little.

"What's the matter?" he asks, with an edge to his voice.

I try to tell him that I don't want his help anymore, but the words just don't come out.

"Jingo, if I'm going to train you, we have to trust each other."

"Like I trusted you to get me beat up yesterday?" I snap back. I regret it immediately.

"I thought that might be it. Look, mate, you are getting into a very exclusive club. This isn't a school where your parents can pay off the teacher to advance your belts. In my club, you have to know how to fight and how to take a beating. Otherwise, you can get really hurt."

I don't say anything.

"You're right. I should have warned you and asked if it was okay to take you there yesterday. Never happen again, okay?"

His voice is soft and sounds very apologetic. I wonder how much of it is just an act.

"Come to the club and watch a few of us train," he says in the same soft voice. "If you still don't think my martial arts club is for you, I'll drive you home, no questions asked."

"Yeah, okay," I agree. I know I shouldn't, but I figure this is just easier.

We drive back toward where he mugged the biker, and we pull up in front of an old warehouse. It has faded red letters that read *Johnson's Mill* over the front. There's no sign indicating that this is a martial arts club. It's like they just took over an abandoned building. The area is so sketchy that I doubt anyone would phone the cops if they had.

"You have a good knowledge base," Austin tells me as he steps out of the car, "and you can improvise quickly."

I follow him as he heads for the warehouse. There's a very muscular guy standing outside the front door. He looks like a bouncer from a nightclub, or a security guard from a mall. He nods at Austin as we enter, and then he gives me an up and down. Inside, it sounds much like my dojang.

"Last night when you were being tested, most guys would have just fallen to the floor and pleaded for them to stop."

Austin walks through the door, and I see four guys being trained. Two are stretching on a mat, one is hitting a punching bag, and the last is wrestling. Each one has a trainer.

"You instinctively calculated where each man was. Then you quickly sized them up and executed kicks they were not expecting."

I start to feel proud of myself, even though last night I was ashamed of getting my ass kicked. I listen to Austin as he walks to a caged octagon where two men are facing off. The cage looks just like the ones they use in the professional Ultimate Fighting Championships. In the tae kwon do bouts, the rings are made up of mats stuck together by Velcro.

One of the guys in the cage looks about my age, and has a face filled with scars. Along his left arm is a tattoo of a brightly colored python. The other guy is a little older, college age. He's wearing bright red shorts that have the name *Jonny* on the sides.

"In the ring, your kicks will be an asset," Austin continues, "but you aren't going to have easy wins unless you can improve your ground game."

A bearded guy approaches Austin and says, "I hear you're in charge. I want to enter this kid in one of your title fights."

The bearded guy points at the tattooed guy in the ring. The two men are still just staring at each other, and I wonder why they're waiting.

"We call him the Ripper," the bearded guy boasts.

"I scout my own talent. I'm not the guy in charge of fight cards," Austin tells him and points to an office door. "You need to talk to Jared."

The bearded guy turns to walk toward the office, until Austin calls him back.

"Let me see him fight," Austin says, "and maybe I'll put in a good word."

A bell rings and the whole gym erupts into cheers and whistles. This is so different from my tae kwon do academy that, at first, I'm very uncomfortable. Everyone crowds around the caged octagon as the two fighters circle one another. There are bloodstains on the mat, and neither of the fighters is wearing any gear. No gloves, no footpads, no body guards and no helmets. It looks more like a throw-down than a martial arts match.

Whenever Jonny steps in too close, Ripper kicks out with his long legs to maintain distance. Neither man is close enough for a real power blow, and it makes me wonder what makes Ripper so great.

Jonny is patient. He doesn't lunge or attempt to catch the leg. He simply circles and backs away whenever Ripper kicks.

Then Jonny moves. He's fast, and it looks like Ripper is caught off guard. Jonny leaps into the air and punches downward as he lands. It looks like a move from a video game, but he gets Ripper right on the shoulder. Now he's in close. Jonny goes to throw another punch, and Ripper pivots to dodge. Only Jonny isn't punching, it's just a fake. Instead he kicks low, right behind Ripper's knee.

Even before Ripper can go down, Jonny grabs him around the waist. Ripper tries to push him off, but Jonny throws him to the ground. Within seconds Jonny has Ripper mounted and is going for an arm bar.

Ripper kicks up, and he's flexible enough to land a blow on Jonny's head. It's hard, and Jonny loses his grip on the arm, letting Ripper land a few pounds in his kidneys. Suddenly Ripper has his legs wrapped around Jonny's waist, and the mount is broken. Jonny recovers fast and gets Ripper in a headlock. It's old-school, but Ripper's face goes red from lack of oxygen. He's not tapping out, and no one is stopping the fight. Jonny seems to squeeze tighter the longer it goes on. Ripper starts to feel around Jonny's face, until he finds one of Jonny's cuts.

Jonny lets out a cry as Ripper digs his thumbnail into a cut just below Jonny's cheek. Both of Jonny's hands go to his face, and Ripper gives him a hard back kick that sends him to the mat. Then he's on top, in the mount, and there's a devastating ground-and-pound. No one stops it.

"Get it?" Austin asks me as he gives the bearded man two thumbs up.

"No," I have to admit.

"This is the kind of fighter you meet in our matches. What kind of trainer would I be if I let you enter the ring when you couldn't even take the simple pound from last night?"

"I couldn't beat this guy," I say to him.

"Not now. You lost last night and have some nasty bruises. Now we know what to improve in order to make you a winner. Your ground game."

chapter twelve

The last place I want to be is my dojang. If I had told Austin I was still going, chances are he would have told me it was a waste of energy. Or maybe he would have said that any extra training is good for my game. Austin is a hard guy to read.

To me it feels like a waste of time. Are they really teaching me anything helpful? I'm in the dojang, and I'm sparring with a partner. Jason is a cocky guy who's always making sarcastic comments, and I'll admit that he makes me laugh. What bugs me about him now is that he's the same height, weight and belt level as me. Whenever I spar, I normally get partnered with him because it's "even." I'm starting to see why I never advance.

Turn kick, step-in turn kick, back kick. Side kick, front kick, front kick. These are the combos that we have been taught for the last ten years. As Jason and I spar, I start to see openings where I could win. I fake a punch, and Jason turns his body slightly to dodge, but that leaves his lower leg open. In tae kwon do we never hit below the belt, so this isn't seen as a weakness. Without even thinking about it, I kick behind his kneecap, and he goes down like a rock. Master Jong comes running over.

"What happened?"

"Jinho kicked my leg!" Jason growls as he pulls his leg into his chest.

Master Jong looks at me, as if he's confused and doesn't know what to say. I can hear him muttering *This isn't like you* without him even having to say it.

"It was an accident," I lie. I can tell that Jason doesn't believe me, and I'm betting Master Jong doesn't either, but they still act as though they do.

"*Cha rutt!*" Master Jong says to us, and we stand at attention.

"*Kyung yet!*" he says, and we bow to one another. As we come up from our bow, Jason and I shake hands, and I apologize again.

"No worries," Jason says to me. "It happens."

I watch Jason limp to the benches, where some of the parents are watching. His mom is there, and she glares at me. I look down and away, but I'm not concerned that she'll phone my mom. Even if she did, my mom needs me to translate into Korean.

"Jinho!" Master Jong calls me back to the present. "Pair up with Philip for a bit."

I nod and go over to where Philip is standing. He's holding two targets, which basically look like padded badminton rackets. We take up fighting stances facing each other, and he holds out one target. "Step one, round kick, then front kick. On the round kick, keep your body at a forty-five degree angle to the target," Philip says.

"If a guy wanted to take me down, don't I make myself completely open to it?" I ask.

"There are no takedowns in tae kwon do. You know that," Philip says, as if that's a real answer.

"Okay, but what about on the street? I'm brawling with a guy, and I face my hips to him. What's stopping him from lunging out, grabbing my waist and throwing me to the ground?"

Philip stares at me as though I just insulted his girlfriend. "Where's all this coming from?"

"Just asking." I get ready to kick. I'm waiting for Philip to hold out the target, but instead he steps up to me and opens my uniform.

"What's this?" he asks, pointing at the bruises on my chest. "Did someone beat you up?"

My instinct is to lie and say no. If I admit that I've been in a fight, I may wind up telling him too much. It wasn't that I was ever specifically told not to talk about the fight club, but I just have a feeling that Austin wouldn't want me to.

"I got jumped," I finally say. It isn't a complete lie.

"Did you tell your mom? Or get checked out at a hospital? Are you okay?"

He's still holding my shirt, and now I'm getting upset. If anything was broken, there's no way I'd be able to stand up right now. And if I was hurt, it would mean the training in this school really sucks.

"I took care of it," I tell him forcefully, imagining that my eyes have that same stone-cold stare as Craig's. Philip loosens his grip on my shirt, and I know that I've intimidated him. It feels good.

"If you need to go slower, just say so," Philip says as he holds out the target.

These are kicks that I've been doing for most of my life, and I realize that I don't even think about them when I do them.

Master Jong always talks about being in the moment, and right now I am as far from the moment as one can get.

"Why can't I spar?" I ask.

"Because Master Jong wants you working on technique. You accidentally kicked Jason's leg, so you need to practice control."

It bugs me the way he says "accidentally," as if he's implying that I did it on purpose. I mean, I did do it on purpose, but there's no reason why he should be accusing me of that. I continue to kick in the pattern, hitting the targets perfectly. Out of the corner of my eye, I see Jason still sitting on the bench holding his leg to his chest.

"Can you ground fight?" I ask Philip as I kick the target.

"You've been watching too much UFC," Philip says. Is he avoiding the question?

"So you can't," I say.

"Actually, I take on-campus judo on Saturdays. I may go to Victoria and enter a mixed martial arts tournament next month."

That surprises me, and I miss a kick.

"Less chat," Philip says.

"Why Victoria?" I ask him, wondering why he wouldn't just get involved in a tournament here. It suddenly makes me feel important to know that I could hook him up if he needs the contacts.

"In Vancouver MMA is against the law—something about prize-fighting. In Victoria, it's legal. Matches are regulated. Doctors are present, the referee is trained and fighters get in trouble if they break the rules."

I step in and round-kick the pad Philip's holding. Then I front-kick from the same spot.

"Forty-five degree angle," Philip reminds me.

"I thought MMA had no rules," I say to him as I prepare to kick again.

"Underground MMA has no rules." As Philip says this, I can hear the suspicion growing in his tone. "MMA is a sport that takes a lot of skill—and it is highly regulated to keep it safe as well."

I step forward, even though he clearly isn't ready, and I round-kick the pad.

"*Cha rutt*," he says, and I stand at attention. "*Kyung yet.*" We bow.

He walks me off the dojang floor and sits with me. "Jinho, if you got beat up, I completely understand why you're angry. But violence is not a solution, and taking it out on your classmates isn't either."

"So what is?" I ask him gruffly.

He sits with his legs crossed, and I do the same.

"We'll meditate awhile on the code of tae kwon do. Today, we'll think about what integrity means to us."

He closes his eyes and breathes in through his nose and out through his mouth. I also close my eyes, but instead of thinking about integrity, I think about getting into a more physical martial art.

chapter thirteen

My mom thinks I've gone to school, but
really I'm going to the warehouse to see
if Austin's around. I still feel a bit weird
accepting his training, but I also can't help
but feel stoked about being a part of his
world. Fast cars, respect from strangers
and even the danger fill me with excitement. He could have picked anyone at
that tournament, but I was the one he saw
promise in.

I go to Austin's warehouse, the one that he had taken me to yesterday. There's a big guy guarding the door. It's the same guy as yesterday, so I'm assuming he'll remember me. I walk up to the door and nod, and he moves to block me. A day or two ago, I would have walked away. But what can this guy do that's worse than the beating I took the other night?

"Where do you think you're going?" he asks me.

A little voice in my head tells me to turn away. But I'm just so sick of everyone telling me what to do that I wind up going chest to chest with this guy.

"I'm going inside," I tell him, though my voice isn't as brave as I feel.

"What's going on, mate?" Austin appears at the door.

I'm still staring at this guy, and he's staring back at me.

"You know this punk?" he asks Austin.

"Yeah. Yeah, I do." Austin pats my shoulder, and I back down. It bugs me that this glorified security guard smiles as though I'm the lucky one.

"Why are you here?" Austin asks as we head into the club. "I assumed you weren't interested."

"Didn't feel like school today...," I start to say but stop when we get inside. The training areas have been disassembled, and the equipment is gone. The octagon is still there, but now there are wooden bleachers being constructed around it.

"There's going to be a match tonight. The Ripper challenged our top fighter," Austin says.

I nod, thinking about the show he put on for us yesterday. I wonder how I'd do against him.

"If you're up for it, you can watch tonight."

I nod and try not to look impressed.

"Even better"—Austin's face has that cocky smirk—"you could have your debut fight. Not against the Ripper, but someone more your speed. You could be the undercard."

I don't say anything at first, and a million excuses are rushing through my mind. I know I should say no to this, but I need to know if I really am a fighter. Besides, if Philip can do MMA, then there's nothing wrong with me doing it.

"Yeah, okay." I can't believe the words as they come out of my mouth.

"Awesome. You need to know a few things before tonight." As Austin speaks, we walk around the room. Men are working everywhere to get ready for tonight.

"First, there are no rules. This is a competition to see which man is toughest."

"Okay," I say as I step over someone's open toolbox. I notice we seem to be heading toward a closed door at the back.

"There are no doctors, and no one to patch you up if you're sloppy enough to get hurt. Bring someone who can take you home if that becomes necessary."

I nod as we get to the door. Austin opens it, and inside is the scarred man I saw at the house the other day. I feel a shard of fear penetrate my chest, and my breathing becomes heavy. This time I make a point of not looking at him at all.

"He wants a bout," Austin says matter-of-factly to his boss.

"First dan black, and he thinks he's ready? Can he ground and pound?"

Austin shakes his head. "He can stay off the ground. He's got knockout potential."

"He'll make interesting odds," the bald guy says as he picks up a clipboard. I have no idea what that even means. "What's your name?"

I open my mouth to speak, but Austin quickly says, "Flying Feet." He smiles at me. "Everyone has a fight name."

chapter fourteen

"Yeah, I'm still not feeling well, so my mom wants me to cancel my tutoring lesson," I say into my cell phone. The lie escapes my lips more easily than it had the first time.

"Okay, Jinho, but if you think you're going to cancel next week, I need more notice...," my tutor scolds me before we say goodbye and hang up.

This leaves me with a free hour before my mom expects me home. I'm feeling a little worried about my fight tonight, especially since I have to bring someone in case I get hurt. There's Kyle, but I can't trust him not to brag to the whole school. If Sara finds out, she'll go directly to my mom. What really bugs me is that I am almost eighteen. I can make my own decisions.

I had called my tutor from the basketball court on the school grounds. A couple of kids are playing one-on-one, and I consider joining them. As I approach them, a ball flies just past my head. I turn and see Craig with his friends.

"Think you can beat me twice?" he asks me.

I turn to leave, as I always do when Craig gets in my face. Then I remember the beating I took, and how that pain didn't last. I remember the lessons Austin gave me and his advice on turning fear into respect. One thing is for certain: Craig does not respect me.

"Not my fault if you suck," I say as I turn to face him and his friends.

Craig smiles and steps up to me. We're chest to chest. This is normally when people back down from him. It's hard to breathe, but I'm telling myself that it's from excitement, not fear. One of his friends is running to get the stray ball.

"We'll settle this with a game of twenty-one," Craig says. "You against me. You get first shot."

I don't even respond, and Craig is already standing to the side of the net. I was ready for a fight and can't help but wonder why Craig isn't throwing down with me. The ball is thrown to me as I walk slowly to the three-point line. I bounce the ball and look at the net. Is this really happening? Is Craig not the fighter we all thought he was?

I take my throw, and it swooshes through the hoop. I'm good at this, and I'm fairly sure I can beat Craig. My second throw I score, and then as my third throw goes in, Craig and Nathan jump for the ball. I'm now five points ahead, but everything can change once the ball goes live.

Craig scoops the ball into his hands and immediately gets his back to me. I hold my arms out to cover him, pressing my chest into his back as close as I can without touching him. As I hear the ball thud against the cement, I also feel Craig's elbow punch into my stomach. This is the second time he's done this to me. I'm knocked back, and Craig goes for the shot.

"Foul!" I shout as he dunks.

"I didn't see anything," one of the other guys says.

"Me neither." Another guy laughs.

There's no teacher to take my side, so what can I do but accept that this is how the game will be played? I realize now that we are going to fight, but the fight will be hidden inside a basketball game. I know he expects me to back down, to run away, but I'm energized. I no longer fear Craig. I no longer respect him.

I get up, and Craig takes the three-point line. He free-throws and gets his first shot. It's now 4–5, with me still one point ahead. Everything can change with this next shot. He lines things up and smiles to his buddies. He throws the ball, and it hits the rim. It's not going in, so I take two steps forward and jump for it.

Craig was expecting this, and from the corner of my eye, I see him rushing at me. His fist is up, and he's going to punch me. What he doesn't know is that I wasn't really going for the ball. I side-kick instead. As Craig rushes toward me, my kick connects with his chest. I hear him huff as his legs are swept from underneath him. He hits the ground, and I grab the ball from the air. As he stares at me in disbelief, I dribble the ball twice and make a shot. It goes in.

"Four to six now," I tell him as I wait for him to make a move.

Craig gets up, and I can see his friends waiting for him to give a command. I'm wondering if they'll all jump me, or if Craig will just take me on himself. He walks up to me, smiling the whole while, and then someone throws him the ball.

"Nice shot," he says as he pushes the ball into my chest.

I'm a little confused, but I keep in mind Austin's advice. If Craig fears me, he respects me. If he respects me, he won't want to fight me. I dribble the ball a few times and breathe steadily. Craig is standing near the basket just in the key. I make my shot, and it goes in. I do this two more times, and the ball goes live.

This time I'm ready to play the game Craig's way. I stay light on my feet and wait for Craig to get the ball. I come in close again, knowing he'll try to elbow me. He does, but I move to the side. His elbow connects with air, and I kick his feet out from under him. As he goes down, I scoop the ball, dribble to the three-point line and then shoot. We are now 9–6.

This time he isn't getting up. He's staying on the ground, with his face turning red. At first I wonder if I pushed too far, that maybe I should have just walked away. Then I remember what Austin taught me, and I step up to Craig.

"You had enough?" I can hear in my voice that the fear is gone.

Craig slowly rises, and I'm ready to fight him. Tonight I have my first cage match, and I can consider this my practice. He walks up to my chest, and I make sure to stand as tall as I can so he has to look up to face me. This time it's me who smiles.

"You're pretty brave," he says. He's still staring at me, and I'm not backing away. I can hear his crew starting to surround me.

"Give me one good reason why I shouldn't pound you into this earth," he says.

"Because you can't," I say.

chapter fifteen

My schedule for today:
  6 AM: wake up and do homework
  8 AM: go to school
  4 PM: finish school and study
  6 PM: tae kwon do
  7 PM: English tutor
  8 PM: math tutor
  9 PM: dinner
  10 PM: study and homework
  Midnight: get to bed

Somewhere in there I need to make room for: 7 PM: MMA fight.

I canceled again on my tutor, and he told me again that with such short notice he still has to charge me. No way I'm arguing with him, or my mom will ask why he's so upset. She may not speak English, but she does speak anger. I told him we'd still pay him, and that I wanted to take off all next week.

"My mom's gonna kill me if she finds out," I mutter as we approach the warehouse.

"What are you, twelve? Mamas' boys don't win fights, so stop being a mama's boy. You can't be thinking about that," Craig says.

His crew is close on our heels. He's the perfect person to bring with me to the fight. Even if he tells everyone he knows at school, none of his friends hang out with mine. And Craig is willing to do just about anything to be here. Even if it means pretending to be my friend. I remember how excited the girls were when they saw me with the Camaro. Now I understand that the fight is to Craig what the car was to the girls.

I nod my head, and we walk up to the door. This time the bouncer gives me a smirk and lets me inside without an argument. It occurs to me that his lack of aggression toward me is perhaps an indication that I may be in trouble. Maybe he feels sorry for me.

As we enter the building, I hear cheering. Beneath the cheers, if you really listen, there's the sound of fists and feet and bodies slamming on the hard floor. I'm trying not to look impressed as I search for Austin. Craig has his gaze locked on the two guys in the ring. One of them is pressing the other against the cage. Both the men are covered in blood.

"Where's the ref?" Craig asks.

"There is none," I say flatly. I can see Austin making his way through the crowd toward me.

"G'day, Jingo! Glad you could make it."

There's an edge to his voice. "You're up after this round. Are you ready?"

I'm wearing sweats and a T-shirt, though I have my tae kwon do uniform in my bag. I pause for a moment to answer, but Austin shouts in my ear, "Are you ready?"

"Yeah," I say.

"Look, Jingo." Austin has his hands on my chest. "I'm putting my reputation on the line here. You get in there and mess up, it's bad for both of us."

I nod. Craig comes up behind me motioning his crew to get closer to me.

"Let's tape up your hands and get you ready."

We go into the back room, where Austin starts to wrap my hands in bandages.

"What's this for?" I ask.

"Unbelievable. Did they teach you nothing at your tae kwon do school? This is so when you're pounding the guy, you don't break your wrist. The gloves I'm going to give you protect your knuckles but will leave your thumbs and palms free for ground fighting."

I nod, and he looks me directly in the eyes.

"Jingo, you have to try and stay off the ground. This guy gets you down, and you're toast. You just don't have the experience yet. Push him against the cage, knock the air out of his lungs and use your knees and elbows."

I nod again, and he hands me the gloves. Then he takes out a jar of Vaseline and rubs some on my face.

"This will make you slippery, so that when you get hit you won't get cut. Are you planning on getting hit?"

I shake my head.

"Jingo, can you talk?"

"Yeah."

"Remember this. You owe this guy no respect. He doesn't deserve any! You are the one who deserves his respect, and today you will teach him why. Get it?"

"Respect is fear," I say.

"Louder!"

"Respect is fear!" I say more forcefully.

"That will have to do."

Austin checks my hands and pats my shoulder. I put on my tae kwon do pants, and then start to put on the shirt. Austin stops me.

"Why not just glue handles on your body to make yourself easier to throw down? I had a feeling this would happen."

He throws me a pair of red fight shorts, and as I change into them, I hear him mumble, "At least you were smart enough to wear a cup."

I slide the gloves onto my fists.

"No robe, right?" It's more of a statement than a question. When I don't answer, he walks to a metal locker and reaches inside.

"You can wear mine," he tells me, throwing me a black cotton robe. As I slip it on, I feel something change in me. I feel like a fighter.

I enter the arena and hear the crowd cheer. The announcer's voice booms over loudspeakers set into the ceiling. "Introducing, in his debut fight, standing at five feet eight inches, weighing in at one hundred and forty pounds"—the crowd goes ballistic—"Flying Feet!"

Austin pushes me forward, and I start to jog to the octagon. It's hard not to get swept up in the excitement of it all and believe that this is the recognition a fighter should get. I'm not here representing my school or my master. I'm here to prove that I'm better than whoever steps into the ring with me. As I climb in through a door that gets shut behind me, I raise my hands and give a few punches in the air.

"Don't overdo it," Austin tells me with a smile on his face from the other side of the cage.

"And in the other corner"—the announcer's voice is menacing—"standing at six feet five inches and weighing in at two hundred and twenty pounds…"

The most muscular guy I've ever seen walks slowly out of the other change room. He's surrounded by three equally big men, and his stone-cold stare bores into me.

For a moment, my heart stops beating and all I want to do is go home.

"Bone Crusher!" the announcer yells, and the crowd goes silent.

"This guy is a good ground fighter," Austin tells me. "His MO is to ground and pound, and he doesn't care if you tap out or get knocked out."

This is information I could have used before I agreed to the match.

Craig, who's been sitting on a cage-side seat, jumps up to the ring beside Austin. "Look at me," he says forcefully.

"Who the—?" Austin starts, but I ignore him and stare at Craig. He's got that same stone-cold stare as Bone Crusher. I stare back and memorize it. I start to understand that all along, Craig was never fearless. He just knows how to pretend that he's fearless. It's all in that emotionless gaze fighters have. As long as I can mimic Craig's, I can have it too.

I turn and face my opponent, who's still staring at me. I pound my gloves together and stare back. Although I can still hear Austin talking to me, it's as if he's in a dream. My head is in the moment...it's just Bone and me.

"Use your legs to keep him from taking you down," Austin says. "If he grabs you, get him against the cage. Push when he pulls. Pull when he pushes—"

"You win this fight," Craig interrupts, "and no one can push you around again. You beat this guy, and you are king."

"Thanks for the tips, mate," Austin says to Craig as he signals to one of the bouncers. Craig is escorted back to his seat. "But I'll handle things from here."

Austin grabs my shoulders and holds tight. "When Bone Crusher entered the arena, everyone went silent. They did so because they fear him. They respect him. No one here respects you. Tonight, you have the chance to earn it."

In tae kwon do, I love it when I take a kick to the head or when some guy punches me in the chest. When I can take some other guy's hit, it makes me feel tough.

But there are always moves I stop myself from using because they are frowned upon in my sport. Tonight I am free to win any way I can. With any move I see open to me.

chapter sixteen

My only chance is to get a knockout.
Bone's only chance is to submit me on
the ground. He has a longer arm reach.
I have a longer leg reach. I'm outweighed
by almost a hundred pounds. I have to
stop myself from thinking any of these
things as I dance around him.

Each time he reaches for me, I kick out
with my leg. Front kicks work well to push
him back, and so far I'm too fast for him to
grab me. He steps in, and I land a punch,

and even though I'm wearing gloves, I can still feel his jaw on my knuckles. He stumbles to the side, and I move back.

"Follow through! Leg kicks!" I hear Austin shout at me from the side.

Bone leaps at me now, and for such a heavy guy, his agility surprises me. I feel his hands reaching around my waist, and I know he's about to go for the takedown. Quickly I lift my knee, connecting with his jaw, and then an elbow to the back of his head. He's off me and stumbling again. Maybe I can still win.

I side-kick him to get him off balance, and he's moving toward the wall of the cage. Then I rush at him to push him against the mesh and knock the wind out of him. I hear Austin shouting at me to stop, but every instinct tells me this is the right move.

By the time I catch Bone's smile, it's too late for me. At the cage he ducks down and gets my waist. Within seconds I feel my body slamming against the ground, and it's me who has the wind knocked out. He's got me in his front mount, sitting on my chest, and I feel a flurry of punches to my head. He's not wearing gloves, and the sound of bone on bone echoes in my ears. I'm desperate to tap out, and he keeps trying to grab my fist to go for the arm bar. I remember the fight I saw with Ripper, and I use his leg move. I'm just as flexible, so I hook my feet behind Bone's neck. He reaches for them as they press on his jugular. I take that split second to punch at his kidneys, and I manage to knock him off balance with my feet on his back.

If I was better at ground fighting, I could probably do a reverse mount and try to pin him. I'm not, so I scramble to get out from beneath him and back on my feet. He's up fast as well. I can feel blood dripping from my chin, but I'm not sure where it's coming from. He's got marks on his neck from where my feet were pressed. Austin is still yelling at me, demanding that I go for the knockout.

Bone rushes me, his anger taking over. Rather than moving away, I leap forward and land with a punch to the top of his head. There's a crack, and he's dazed. Spinning my body around, I leap up with one foot and bring the other down in a flying axe kick. I land right at the top of his forehead, and the crowd goes insane. Bone staggers, drops to his knees and then keels over onto the mat. Suddenly the crowd is silent.

Respect is mine.

"We have a winner!" I hear the announcer yell as I return to my corner.

Austin was sitting with Craig, and now he rushes back to the octagon. The door opens, and suddenly I realize how exhausted I am.

"Jingo! I knew you could do it!" Austin holds my arm up again, as a show to the crowd that his fighter has won.

Standing outside the main office, I see the bald guy from the other day. The one who grabbed me by the scruff of my neck. The one who held me in the circle. The one who punched and kicked me until

I couldn't get back up. He has his arms crossed, and there's a smile on his face.

I pull my arm free of Austin's grip and give him a little shove. Craig is still sitting in his seat, maybe too stunned to come congratulate me. I give Austin the same glare that I gave Bone Crusher.

"My name is Jin*HO*."

Austin smiles and slaps my shoulder. "That's the spirit I've been waiting to see."

chapter seventeen

It's still dark outside when my alarm goes off. I'm lying in bed. I've hardly slept at all, and I'm counting the hours since I last took two Tylenols. The bottle says not to exceed two tablets every six hours, and I took two not even three hours ago. My head is pounding, and my cheek is throbbing. I've never felt this kind of pain before.

But I'm a winner, I remind myself. This is how it feels to win.

Getting in last night without my mom seeing me was tough. I had to sneak in the front door, tiptoe up the stairs and then call to her that I was home. I told her I had a headache and that I needed the lights off so I could sleep. It wasn't a complete lie. I just didn't tell her how I got the headache. She said that was okay, so long as I got up early this morning to do homework. Now I have a good excuse for taking off before she wakes up.

I crawl out of bed and take off my shirt. The bruises from my first beating have faded to a light shade of blue. But now new bruises are all over my chest and back, often running into the old ones. There are cuts on my face, and I'm a little worried about them getting infected. I didn't exactly wash up all that well yesterday.

But I'm a winner, I remind myself again.

I grab a set of clean clothes and head for the shower. My mom sleeps like a rock, so there's not that much chance of waking her. Still, I'm extra quiet. I stand under the shower and the dried blood swirls down the drain. None of the wounds reopen, but when I dry off, it leaves a faint red stain on the white towel. I decide to take the towel with me and throw it out on my way to school.

I go down the stairs quietly, checking to see if my mom has woken up while I was in the shower. She hasn't, so I head quickly to the fridge, grab a container of kimchi and take it with me to eat on the bus. People will glare at me because they aren't used to the smell, but I gotta eat something. I decide to hang out at the park before school opens.

When I'm finally walking through the halls at school, none of the boys want to meet my eyes. Can't blame them, considering how I look. My right cheek is bruised and both my eyes are black. They hurt a little, but I consider them battle wounds.

"What happened to you?" Kyle asks when he sees me.

"I was in a special mixed martial arts

tournament last night," I say in a hushed voice.

"You were not," he says. I don't respond, and he asks, "You were?"

Before I can answer, Sara pushes in front of Kyle.

"What happened?" She gently strokes my face. Her eyes closely examine my bruises.

"That trainer put him in an MMA fight last night," Kyle says with a hint of admiration in his voice. "Can I come next time?"

"You can't tell Master Jong," I say to Sara.

"How are you going to explain your face?" Sara asks. "What did your mom say this morning?"

I see Craig walking fast toward us. He's alone, which isn't like him.

"We gotta talk," Craig interrupts us as he pushes his way in front of Kyle.

I'm thankful for the distraction and shrug as I walk away with him. Kyle is speechless, as is Sara. They must be imagining all sorts of reasons for my behavior—fighting, skipping school and now hanging out with the school tough guy.

"You need to talk to your buddy Austin. He spotted me a hundred bucks last night, and I lost it all on a bet."

"But I won," I say, feeling confused.

"Didn't bet on your fight. I bet against the Ripper."

I find myself wondering why Austin would take his bet, considering Craig is a friend of mine. Well, he's not exactly a friend, but he is as far as Austin knows.

"Tell Austin he needs to forget about it," Craig demands.

He has that killer stare, but his voice barely hides his fear. He's panicking, and I'm the one he feels safe confronting. Even after my bout last night, he has no respect for me. I shove him hard in the chest. I'm sick to death of people telling me how to live my life.

"Maybe next time you'll bet on the right fighter!"

His eyes are wide now, and he's no longer giving me the tough act.

"Come on, man! My family is on welfare, and I can't get that kind of cash," he whines.

There are people starting to gather around us. No one has ever stood up to Craig before. I'm thinking how cool it would be if I finished with a side kick square in his chest.

"Is there a problem, boys?" Mr. Quinton asks. He's one of the bigger teachers, and Craig actually respects him, so he immediately backs off.

"No problem." Craig walks away.

Mr. Quinton watches me for a second, and I consider staring him down. I'm still pumped, but I know that I have to lie low for a while. I start to walk away, but Mr. Quinton grabs my arm.

"Did he do this to you?" he asks me.

"No," I say. "I had a bike accident."

Mr. Quinton stares at my knuckles, and I know he thinks I'm lying.

"Gotta get to class," I say, yanking myself free of his grasp.

The last place I feel like being is at school. As soon as the bell rings and the halls start to empty, I duck out one of the exit doors. I call Austin to see if we can do some training.

"Glad you called. We need to meet," he tells me.

There's an edge to his voice that makes me think about the night he introduced me to the scarred man. "Uh, yeah. Sure," I say with less confidence than I want to convey.

"Meet me at First and Main. You'll see my car, I'm sure."

chapter eighteen

I hang up and go to the bus stop. There's a couple of guys throwing kicks around, and I wonder what Jackie Chan movie is playing at the local second-run theater. Guys always get like this after seeing a martial arts movie, like they've somehow become experts.

"Jinho!" Sara is running toward me.

"I have somewhere to be. I really don't have time," I tell her.

She looks as if she's about to cry. "Are you okay?"

"Why wouldn't I be?" I ask harshly.

"You've been skipping school, for one thing," she reminds me.

I see my bus coming. "You won't tell anyone," I say to her firmly.

She says nothing, and I know that she's planning on going to tell someone. "Promise me you won't say anything!" I say harshly enough that the two karate kids stop to watch us, as if they could step in and stop me if I got violent.

"Okay," she agrees quietly as the bus pulls up to the stop. I get on, with no more words for Sara. I'm just hoping she doesn't ruin this for me.

Industrial Avenue is in another warehouse district. No one in the neighborhood would complain about a fight club. I see Austin's car a few buildings down on Industrial Avenue, so I jog to it.

He's sitting inside the car and gets out as I approach.

"Jinho." He pats my back as I walk up to him. "Mate! Look at those bruises! You look awesome!"

It makes me feel pretty good to hear him say that. He walks toward a building that looks as though it's ready for demolition. A large man stands guard outside. Austin nods to him, and he moves aside to let us in.

There's another caged octagon and people setting up wooden bleachers. Inside the octagon is a middle-aged bald man exchanging kicks with Ripper.

"The school has moved," Austin says. "We'll be here for tonight's bouts. I have some good news for you. You're the main event."

I'm only half-listening as I watch the two guys in the ring kicking each other's shins. The cracks echo in the high rafters, as does the sound of the punch one guy slams into his opponent's jaw.

"You remember the Ripper?" Austin faces the octagon. "He's the guy you'll be fighting."

Ripper lands a kick square in the other guy's chest, but is caught by a tackle to the waist. He's pushed against the cage, and Baldy holds him tight. Baldy is pushing his shoulder into Ripper's chest, squeezing the air out. Ripper is struggling to get out but only manages to get one arm free.

"Watch this," Austin says with a smile plastered on his face.

Ripper grabs a cut in Baldy's cheek with his thumb and then places his fingers behind his head. As he squeezes, his thumb rips open the wound and blood starts to pour out.

"Now the other guy has to be careful. If blood gets in his eye, he could go blind."

All it takes after that is for Ripper to kick hard to Baldy's chest. Baldy stumbles backward, and then he's knocked to the ground by a quick kick behind the kneecap. Ripper mounts him, grabs his wrist in an arm bar and begins to pull. Baldy is tapping surrender, but Ripper continues to pull until Baldy lets out a bloodcurdling scream and several men enter the ring to pull them apart.

"You're on tonight at nine. Don't be late," Austin tells me and starts to walk away.

"No way," I say as Baldy is carried out of the ring. Ripper is laughing like a maniac.

"There's no discussion, mate." Austin is emotionless as he tells me this. I consider leaving and losing his number, but I know he can find me. Maybe I do need to tell someone about this.

"And don't even think about going to the cops," he says with a smirk. "Think about it. You're seventeen, which makes you very close to being an adult. You fought, willingly, in an illegal martial arts tourney. What are you going to tell them? Not to mention immigration. Aren't you here on a student visa? How would your mom feel if you were kicked out of Canada?"

I shrug. It's starting to occur to me just how deep into this I am.

"And your friend Craig"—Austin puts his hands on my shoulders and squeezes them—"he owes me money that I know he can't afford to pay back."

"He's not even my friend" is all I can think of to say.

"So you won't mind if I go and collect? Think Craig can take me?"

I know he can't. I'm not even sure if I can, though there's a part of me that wants to try. I can feel my temper rising, but I have to keep it in check.

Austin pushes me in the chest, and I stumble back toward the door. "Save the temper for the ring," he says. "It's the only thing going for you right now."

Trouble has caught up to me in a way that I can't handle. I walk out of the warehouse and head back toward the bus stop. I feel my cell buzzing and consider ignoring it. Probably Kyle wondering why I ditched class. The phone stops buzzing, but starts again a minute later. This goes on as I'm walking down the street until I finally answer it. My hands are shaking.

"Hey, Jinho. It's Philip from Jong's dojang."

"Hey, Philip."

"I was hoping you and I could get together before class tonight." He's always so enthusiastic when he speaks. I feel angry with him for sounding so carefree.

"Why?" I ask quickly.

"Sara called." There's a pause. I know what he's saying. I'm disappointed that Sara betrayed my trust, but I'm also glad that I have someone I can go to for help. Philip understands MMA, so maybe he'll have some advice.

"Okay," I say.

"Meet me at the Starbucks on the corner near the dojang."

"Thanks." I hang up and start walking.

chapter nineteen

Philip is seated outside the café at one of the metal tables. He's got a cup of coffee already and is writing in a notebook. He's dressed in a gray polo shirt with blue jeans. It's strange to see him outside the dojang. He takes one look at me and frowns.

"What the hell happened to you?" he asks.

"MMA," I tell him flat out.

"MMA? This doesn't happen in MMA. I go to judo every Saturday morning at the university. Master Jong and my judo instructor are helping me train for MMA, and I've never seen anyone come from a bout looking like you."

I don't know what to say, so I don't say anything.

"In Victoria, the fights are regulated," he continues. "Fighters train hard and show a lot of respect for each other, and we never hurt each other the way you've been hurt."

I'm trying to read him to see if I should tell him what happened. This could backfire if his only response is to go to my mom. I don't think about that as I take a deep breath and spill my guts about everything that has gone on these past few weeks.

"You have to tell your mom," Philip says. So predictable. He's even leaning over the table, his elbows tucked under his chest.

I shake my head and lean in closer to the table, so no one else can hear us speaking. There's only two other people out here—

one loud woman on a cell phone and some guy smoking a cigarette.

"Can't do that." I wonder how to make him understand just how badly I've screwed up. "If I do, my mom will ship me back to Korea to stay with my dad. That can't happen."

He leans back in his seat and shrugs his shoulders. "Jinho, this is really serious." He looks at me as though he thinks my going back to Korea wouldn't be such a bad thing. He shakes his head the way people do when they've just heard something completely ridiculous.

"So, he wants you to fight this guy..."

"Ripper," I remind him.

"Or else he'll beat up your friend."

Philip takes another long sip of his coffee and closes his notebook. "Want me to go talk to him?"

I can tell by his voice that he's only asking because it seems like the right thing for an adult to do. I shake my head, and he nods.

"We can tell Master Jong then. Or the police."

"We can't tell anybody!" I realize that people are now watching. I'm not sure what I expected from Philip. Of course he'd say we need to tell Master Jong or the cops.

"Jinho, I am not going to tell you this is all right."

I feel defeated, as though all my options are gone. No matter what I do, I'm going to get burned.

"I wasn't the one who came to you for help," I say as I stand to leave. I wait for a few seconds, not sure what I'm hoping he'll say.

"No, but Sara did. She wouldn't tell me what was going on, but she was in tears. She begged me to help you."

Anger builds in me as I realize that Sara went to Philip because she doesn't believe I can win. She still thinks I'm a loser, and all because of that stupid tae kwon do tournament last weekend. If she'd seen me fight last night, if she'd seen me beat down that huge guy, she'd know that I am a winner.

That's when I decide I have to enter this last fight. I have to prove to everyone that I'm not some kid who needs protecting. I'm almost a grown man, and I can handle myself. In the ring, and out of it.

"Thanks for helping make this very clear," I say as I head for the bus stop.

"Hold on," Philip calls me back. "Come to tae kwon do tonight, and I'll show you some of the MMA moves I've learned."

I consider his offer. I could use more help, especially if I have to fight the Ripper. I can see in Philip's eyes that he's going to go to Master Jong, and then I'll never get to the bout. If I show up at tae kwon do, Master Jong won't let me leave the dojang. There's some relief in thinking I could let this decision be taken from me. But if I do that, Austin will beat up Craig. He may not be my friend, he may even deserve a good beating, but I don't want to feel responsible for it.

"Sorry," I say to Philip as I leave.

I go back to school and wait off the grounds, where I can have a clear view of the front door. I see people coming out of the school, each one in a rush to get away. There's a group of guys standing at the side of the school, several of them smoking. Craig is in the middle of them, and he's throwing taunts at smaller guys who walk past. I shake my head. Why had I ever thought I could trust him? Why had I been afraid of him? Maybe I should let Austin kick his ass. But then Austin would also make sure I got kicked out of Canada.

When Craig's gang starts to move away from the school, I quickly walk over to him, this time with no fear. Two of his friends step in to stop me, but I slam my shoulder against one and shove the other hard.

"Stop!" Craig commands them, just as they're about to fight back. They give me a look that says I should feel lucky. I give them one that tells them I don't believe them.

"You can breathe easy. I'll fight tonight," I say to Craig.

"What made you change your mind?" he asks.

"Not you," I say. "I'll meet you back here at eight tonight. You're coming with me to the fight."

I walk off, feeling no better about what I have to do. I'm still sore from yesterday, but I have to put that to the back of my mind. The only thing I can concentrate on now is the fight ahead of me.

chapter twenty

This time in the change room, it's just Craig and me. Austin isn't with me for a pep talk, and I'm not expecting him at the ringside either. This time I've brought my own fight shorts, but I don't have gloves, nor do I have a robe. Sweat is already beading on my forehead, and my fingers won't stop shaking.

"You've got nothing to fear," Craig tells me.

I nod as if I believe him.

"You have everything to fear," Austin's voice says at the door.

Austin walks in and stands between the two of us.

"This is how tonight will go. Jinho wins, you're both off the hook. He loses, I come collecting my due. Money from Craig, another fight from Jinho."

"No," I say. "This is how tonight will go: I fight tonight. Win or lose, we're square. Even. I'm out. Craig's out. Period."

I hope my voice sounds braver than I feel.

"Looks like I managed to teach you something after all," Austin says. "You put up a good fight, you're both out. You throw the fight, or don't show up, I come looking for both of you."

Austin turns and swaggers out of the room.

"I guess you can go home," I say to Craig once we're alone.

Craig reaches into a knapsack he's brought and takes out a first-aid kit.

"Lifted from school," he tells me as he takes out the gauze tape.

"Didn't you hear me? You don't have to stay."

"Yes, I do," he says as he begins to wrap my hands in tape. "Don't get me wrong, it isn't as though things have changed between us. I'm here to make sure my debt is cleared."

As Craig speaks, I can't help but think there must be something more. His reasoning rings false. Maybe he's really here because we're becoming friends. Maybe by living the code of tae kwon do—courtesy, integrity, perseverance, self-control and indomitable spirit—I have caused change in Craig. This is what martial arts are about, and what I've been turning my back on.

"You don't put up a good fight in there, and I'll kick your ass," he warns me as he finishes wrapping my hands in the tape.

"You'd better hope that it doesn't come to that," I say.

"My boys are ringside. Things get too ugly, I'm taking off, without you."

The announcer starts his introductions, and I know it's time to go. Craig and I head to the door. Deep breaths. Concentrate on the code of tae kwon do. The code I have spent my whole life not understanding. This will be my guide to victory. Before I enter the gym, I bow. Craig starts walking first, and I follow behind.

The room is chanting my name—my fight name that is. *"Fly-ing Feet! Fly-ing Feet!"* Craig and I approach the octagon, and I see Ripper in his corner. He's staring at me with a smile plastered on his face. Austin is in his corner.

"Never mind him!" Craig says in my ear. "Concentrate on your bout. This is a knockout fight, or I'm going to have to carry you to a hospital. No way I want to do that, so you gotta knock him out!"

One of Craig's boys rushes to my side and Vaselines my face and knuckles. He puts a little too much on, and I'm worried about it getting in my eyes. I grab a towel and pat a little off.

"This guy isn't so tough," I say to Craig.

Then I turn to Ripper, but I glare at Austin. Truth is, my stomach is churning with fear. My feet feel weak, and my chest is heavy.

"You can't show him your fear," Craig says to me. "Even if you are afraid, you have to show him you are confident. It'll confuse him and make him second-guess his every move."

Craig is right—just because I feel the fear doesn't mean I have to show it. They can think I'm confident. And if I convince them, maybe I can convince myself.

The bell rings, and we circle each other around the octagon. He has his fists up, and so do I. Neither of us has on any gloves or shin pads or body armor. Ripper comes at me strong with a flurry of jabs to my face and body. Most of them I dodge, and the few that land just nick me. I use a front kick to push him away, and Ripper tries to grab my leg. I pull it back too quickly for him.

Ripper's smile bugs me, and I find it surprising that he's not missing any teeth. He throws a knifehand strike, and it lands on my ear. There's a ringing sound in my head, and the world spins for just a second. But in the octagon, that second may as well be an hour. He stomps his heel on my foot, and there's a shooting pain up my leg. Broken toe. Can't kick with that foot. I pivot slightly to stay at an angle to him, and Ripper punches me hard in the kidney.

"Fight back!" I can hear Craig screaming at me above the roar of a very pleased crowd.

I spin around with the broken-toe foot in the air, using the heel to kick Ripper hard in the chest. I hear him shout "Ooof!" as he stumbles backward, and I follow up with a superman punch by jumping in the air and directing my fist hard at his forehead. He dodges, and I manage to hit only air.

A bell rings, and the first round is over. Ripper doesn't hear it, or he ignores it, and I feel his fist slam across my cheek. He lingers for a moment to see if I'm also going to continue fighting, and I consider it. I can feel my temper taking over my body.

I want to grab him and throw him down. Punch him repeatedly. Kick him hard.

"*Cha rutt!*" I yell instead. I stand at attention. "*Kyung yet!*" I bow to him and return to my corner, ignoring his laughter.

chapter twenty-one

Craig's buddies are ready with water for me to rinse my mouth and ice packs to cool my head and sweating body. One of them enters the octagon with the first-aid kit and grabs the foot with the broken toe.

"What the hell are you doing?" Craig asks me.

"Fighting with honor," I say. The words in my mouth taste odd, but for the first time in a long while I start to feel whole.

"You're getting your ass kicked," Craig corrects me. "There are no rules in this fight. You can't break a rule that doesn't exist!"

The bell dings, and we're ready to go another round. Ripper leaps into the octagon, and I stand gently on my foot. Craig's buddy taped my broken toe to a good toe, so I can hardly feel it now. I consider for a second what Craig said to me.

"I have rules. I have a code," I tell him as I turn and bow to the Ripper.

The audience is laughing as though I'm acting like a clown. I understand now how far this club has fallen from the tradition of martial arts. I start to feel like a warrior whose duty it is to bring that honor back.

Ripper goes immediately for the takedown. His hands grab at my waist, but I knee him hard in the face. He tries again, and I get an elbow down on his back. Austin must have told him about my weakness, and that it would be easiest to ground-fight me. I try using my front kicks to keep him at a distance, and I strike with punches. He's determined to get me on the ground, and without realizing it, I've moved near the wall of the cage.

In a schoolyard tackle, Ripper's entire body weight slams into me. He wraps his arms around my chest, locking his hands into the mesh of the cage. His head is pressed in the center of my lungs, and I can't breathe. I try to use my knees, but there's no room. I elbow hard to his back, but it's like hitting stone. Craig is behind me, safe on the other side of the cage, yelling to me that I should foot-sweep him. I can feel the world starting to go black as I manage to hook my leg into one of his. Then a little kick...

Air rushes back into my lungs as Ripper loses his balance and falls backward. I follow up quickly with a punch to his head and a kick to his chest. He's on the ground, and Craig is screaming at me to finish him. I could stomp on Ripper's head, really do some damage, but instead I stop. I bow. I wait.

"What are you doing?" Craig wails.

Even though I know it's crazy, I let Ripper stand again. The bell dings, but this time Ripper ignores it.

He flies at me again to get his hands around my waist. He knocks me to the ground, and he's in the mount. I can hear Craig yelling that the bell has gone, but no one is entering the ring to stop us. Ripper is trying to grab my arm, to get me into an arm bar, but I manage to hook my leg over his elbow to weaken his grip. With my other leg, I kick at his kidneys.

With only one free hand, Ripper leans down and puts his forearm over my throat. I pound at his head with my free fist. My foot that's holding his arm slips, and he gets loose for a second. That's all he needs. I feel him grab my wrist, and my arm is almost straight. He elbows me across my face, and now blood is dripping onto the mat. I'm cut, because we didn't grease up my face at the end of round one.

I'm trying to hook my leg over his arm again, and I feel one of his hands on my face. I know I have to throw him off me, but he's managed to hook his legs under my thighs in a butterfly mount. I'm throwing punches. I'm trying kicks. But as I do, I feel his fingers searching for an open cut. I can't think about that as he pulls at my arm to break it. He finds the cut, and a sharp pain shoots into my skull as his nail digs into it. My arm suddenly goes straight, and there's a crack that echoes in the gym. I scream. Ripper isn't going to stop, and I know there's no one here willing to pull him off me.

At that moment we are pulled apart. Three men, all dressed in blue uniforms, yank Ripper off me. They're wearing helmets and wielding batons. I've never been so glad to see the cops in all my life. I lie still on the mat as a paramedic rushes to my side. I can hear him telling me not to move as he checks me out. I start to get a little dizzy, but I can see several men—including Austin—being escorted out in cuffs.

I'm lifted onto a stretcher and whisked outside toward an ambulance. The cold air lifts the pain from my wounds. I breathe deeply. I hear my mom's voice, shouting in Korean, asking if I'm okay. I look over and see her standing with Master Jong, Philip and Sara. I also notice that Craig and his gang are being questioned by the cops.

"You owe him big-time," Philip tells me as he gets as close as the paramedics allow. "Sara gave him the money to pay off his debt so he'd tell her where this was taking place."

I wonder for only a second why Craig would let me go through with the fight if he already had the money to pay off the debt. Then I realize that if I fought, he could keep the money. Had he known that Sara planned to stop the fight, he never would have told her the truth.

"I told Master Jong, who called the police and your mom. I had to tell someone," I hear Philip say to me.

I nod. My voice is gone, and when I try to speak, my throat cramps up.

"Excuse me," Master Jong is saying to one of the paramedics. "This is the boy's mother. She should be with him."

The paramedic nods, and Master Jong pushes Sara ahead. "And this is her translator."

"The mother and the translator can come, but that's all," the paramedic tells us. I feel myself being lifted into the ambulance. My mom and Sara sit at my side.

"Everything will be okay, my boy," Mom tells me with tears streaming down her cheeks.

Sara reaches out for my hand. I give hers a squeeze. I know this isn't over. But whatever happens, I know now that I will have good friends at my side. The ones who taught me the meaning of respect.

Author's Note

At the time this book was written, there was a big controversy over whether or not MMA should be made legal in Vancouver. Technically, all martial arts tournaments are illegal under the prize-fighting law—only boxing is exempt. I wanted to write a book that shed some light on the fact that by not regulating the sport, we are allowing it to flourish underground. In legalized MMA tournaments, there are rules against dangerous moves, a doctor must be present and fighters are held accountable to a licensing board. Underground, fighters can break the rules with little consequence, and doctors may or may not be present. The discussion of whether or not to allow MMA in our community should be less about the morality of violent sport and more about how we can make the sport less about violence and more about talent.

Acknowledgments

I'd like to acknowledge the great editing skills of Sarah Harvey, whose suggestions brought out the best of my writing ability. I'd also like to acknowledge Kang's Tae Kwon Do school in Winnipeg, Manitoba, whose training helped me be a better teenager, and to Peak Performance in Coquitlam, British Columbia, whose training has helped make me a better adult.

James McCann grew up on the icy plains of Manitoba, where he spent most of his teenage years reading comics and training in tae kwon do. In 2002 he came to the West Coast, where he's worked as a book-seller and a workshop leader, mentoring youth in creative writing. When he isn't writing books for teens, James is practicing tae kwon do or going on hikes with his Shih Tzu, Conan. James lives in Coquitlam, British Columbia.

Titles in the Series

orca sports